Playing w
Pres
Robert Loui

The Strange Case of
Dr. Jekyll
and
Mr. Hyde
FOR KIDS
(The melodramatic version!)

For 5-14+ actors, or kids of all ages who want to have fun!
Creatively modified by Brendan P. Kelso
Cover stage illustrated by Shana Hallmeyer
Cover Characters illustrated by Ron Leishman

3 Melodramatic Modifications of Stevenson's novel
for 3 different group sizes:

5-6 actors

7-10 actors

9-14+ actors

Table Of Contents

Foreword .... Pg 4
School, Afterschool, and Summer classes .... Pg 6
Performance Rights .... Pg 6
5-6 Actors .... Pg 8
7-10 Actors .... Pg 36
9-14+ Actors .... Pg 64
Special Thanks .... Pg 94
Sneak Peeks at other Playing With Plays .... Pg 95
About the Author .... Pg 104

To Kenny,
Who is a great alter-ego to my thoughts
and of course had the
BEST Jekyll & Hyde moment with his
Beaver and Lynch incident!

-BPK

Playing with Plays™ - Robert Louis Stevenson's The Strange Case of Dr. Jekyll and Mr. Hyde for Kids

Copyright © 2004-2020 by Brendan P. Kelso, Playing with Plays LLC
Some characters on the cover are ©Ron Leishman ToonClipart.com

All rights reserved. No part of this book may be reproduced in any form or by any electronic or mechanical means, including photocopying, recording, information storage or retrieval systems now known or to be invented, without permission in writing from the publisher, except by a reviewer, who may quote brief passages in a review, written for inclusion within a periodical. Any members of education institutions wishing to photocopy part or all of the work for classroom use, or publishers who would like to obtain permission to include the work in an anthology, should send their inquiries to the publisher. We monitor the internet for cases of piracy and copyright infringement/violations. We will pursue all cases within the full extent of the law.

Whenever a Playing With Plays play is produced, the following must be included on all programs, printing and advertising for the play: © Brendan P. Kelso, Playing with Plays LLC, www.PlayingWithPlays.com. All rights reserved.

CAUTION: Professionals and amateurs are hereby warned that these plays are subject to a royalty. They are fully protected, in whole, in part, or in any form under the copyright laws of the United States, Canada, the British Empire, and all other countries of the Copyright Union, and are subject to royalty. All rights, including professional, amateur, motion picture, radio, television, recitation, public reading, internet, and any method of photographic reproduction are strictly reserved.

For performance rights please see
page 6 of this book or contact:

contact@PlayingWithPlays.com

-Please note, for certain circumstances, we do waive copyright and performance fees.
Rules subject to change

www.PlayingWithPlays.com

Printed in the United States of America
Published by Playing With Plays LLC

ISBN: 9781672836456

Foreword

When I was in high school there was something about Shakespeare that appealed to me. Not that I understood it mind you, but there were clear scenes and images that always stood out in my mind. Romeo & Juliet, "Romeo, Romeo; wherefore art thou Romeo?"; Julius Caesar, "Et tu Brute"; Macbeth, "Double, Double, toil and trouble"; Hamlet, "to be or not to be"; A Midsummer Night's Dream, all I remember about this was a wickedly cool fairy and something about a guy turning into a donkey that I thought was pretty funny. It was not until I started analyzing Shakespeare's plays as an actor that I realized one very important thing, I still didn't understand them. Seriously though, it's tough enough for adults, let alone kids. Then it hit me, why don't I make a version that kids could perform, but make it easy for them to understand with a splash of Shakespeare lingo mixed in? And voila! A melodramatic masterpiece was created! They are intended to be melodramatically fun!

THE PLAYS: There are 3 plays within this book, for three different group sizes. The reason: to allow educators or parents to get the story across to their children regardless of the size of their group. As you read through the plays, there are several lines that are highlighted. These are actual lines from the original book. I am a little more particular about the kids saying these lines verbatim. But the rest, well... have fun!

The entire purpose of this book is to instill the love of a classic story, as well as drama, into the kids.

And when you have children who have a passion for something, they will start to teach themselves, with or without school.

These plays are intended for pure fun. Please DO NOT have the kids learn these lines verbatim, that would be a complete waste of creativity. But do have them basically know their lines and improvise wherever they want as long as it pertains to telling the story. Because that is the goal of an actor: to tell the story. In A Midsummer Night's Dream, I once had a student playing Quince question me about one of her lines, "but in the actual story, didn't the Mechanicals state that 'they would hang us'?" I thought for a second and realized that she had read the story with her mom, and she was right. So I let her add the line she wanted and it added that much more fun, it made the play theirs. I have had kids throw water on the audience, run around the audience, sit in the audience, lose their pumpkin pants (size 30 around a size 15 doesn't work very well, but makes for some great humor!) and most importantly, die all over the stage. The kids love it.

One last note: if you want some educational resources, loved our plays, want to tell the world how much your kids loved performing Shakespeare, want to insult someone with our Shakespeare Insult Generator, or are just a fan of Shakespeare, then hop on our website and have fun:

PlayingWithPlays.com

With these notes, I'll see you on the stage, have fun, and break a leg!

SCHOOL, AFTERSCHOOL, and SUMMER classes

I've been teaching these plays as afterschool and summer programs for quite some time. Many people have asked what the program is, therefore, I have put together a basic formula so any teacher or parent can follow and have melodramatic success! As well, many teachers use my books in a variety of ways. You can view the formula and many more resources on my website at: PlayingWithPlays.com

- Brendan

OTHER PLAYS AND FULL LENGTH SCRIPTS

We have over 25 different titles, as well as a full-length play in 4-acts for theatre groups: Shakespeare's Hilarious Tragedies. You can see all of our other titles on our website here: PlayingWithPlays.com/books

As well, you can see a sneak peek at some of those titles at the back of this book.

And, if you ever have any questions, please don't hesitate to ask at: Contact@PlayingWithPlays.com

ROYALTIES

If you have any questions about royalties or performance licenses, here are the basic guidelines:

1) Please contact us! We always LOVE to hear about a school or group performing our books! We would also love to share photos and brag about your program as well! (with your permission, of course)

2) If you are a group and DO NOT charge your kids to be in this production, contact us about discounted copyright fees (one way or another, we will make this work for you!) You are NOT required to buy a book per kid (but, we will still send you some really cool Shakespeare tattoos for your kids!)

3) If you are a group and DO charge your kids to be in the production, (i.e. afterschool program, summer camp) we ask that you purchase a book per kid. Contact us as we will give you a bulk discount (10 books or more) and send some really cool press on Shakespeare tattoos!

4) If you are a group and DO NOT charge the audience to see the plays, please see our website FAQs to see if you are eligible to waive the performance royalties (most performances are eligible).

5) If you are a group and DO charge the audience to see the performance, please see our website FAQs for performance licensing fees (this includes performances for donations and competitions).

Any other questions or comments, please see our website or email us at:

contact@PlayingWithPlays.com

The 15-Minute or so Jekyll and Hyde for Kids

by Robert Louis Stevenson
Creatively modified by Brendan P. Kelso
5-6 Actors

CAST OF CHARACTERS:

NARRATOR: our funny, all-over-the-place, yet annoying, storyteller
UTTERSON: a lawyer who seeks out the truth
DR. JEKYLL: good scientist with one REALLY bad idea
MR. HYDE: evil – does whatever he wants
[1]**LANYON:** friend of Utterson and Jekyll
[1]**POOLE:** the butler

The same actors can play the following parts:
[1]LANYON and POOLE

NOTE: Both NARRATOR and HYDE are characters that can be improvised throughout the show. NARRATOR is constantly annoying and trying to weave themselves into the story. HYDE takes many liberties, as he does not follow the rules. Be sure to have creative fun with these two characters.

ACT 1 SCENE 1

Story of the Door

(NARRATOR enters)

NARRATOR: Hello, I'll be your narrator this fine sunny Sunday!

(UTTERSON enters)

UTTERSON: Ummm... excuse me... Robert Louis Stevenson clearly made me the narrator.

NARRATOR: *(mocking UTTERSON)* Ummm... you're excused and ya boring! And, you're a lawyer, like anyone's going to trust you!

UTTERSON: Rude!

NARRATOR: Anywhoo... Welcome to London in the 1800s. This is Mr. Utterson.

UTTERSON: Hello.

NARRATOR: Want to hear a fun tale?!

UTTERSON: No.

NARRATOR: Your face is never lighted by a smile. You see that door right there? It has a very odd story.

UTTERSON: You're going to tell me anyway, aren't you?

NARRATOR: We have an audience, have we not?

UTTERSON: Very well, proceed.

NARRATOR: It was 3 am on a winter's morning, and the streets were deserted. And I don't mean filled with cakes and scrumptious treats!

UTTERSON: What?

NARRATOR: Never mind. I saw this man and a young lady walking towards each other. This man ran into her, trampled calmly over and left her screaming on the ground. And then, he started to hobble away!!! Watch! *(HYDE enters and recreates scene with NARRATOR as girl)*

(UTTERSON grabs HYDE)

UTTERSON: No you don't, get back here! *(HYDE stands there very calm)*

HYDE: *(to GIRL)* Listen, I'll pay you a LOT of money if we can just make this... go away.

NARRATOR: OK!

(HYDE exits and returns with money, gives it to "girl", then disappears into the night)

NARRATOR: And he came out of that strange door.

UTTERSON: Hmmm, that is interesting.

NARRATOR: No... what's REALLY interesting is he came out with another man's check. Signed by the very well-known Dr. Jekyll. Look!

UTTERSON: Dr. HENRY Jekyll?!

NARRATOR: The very one! It MUST be blackmail. I've watched the door and the only one who goes in and out is that villainous man!

UTTERSON: Do you know his name?

NARRATOR: Of course, I'm the narrator. Goes by the name of Hyde. And there's something wrong with his appearance, something displeasing, something downright detestable.

(ALL stay onstage)

ACT 1 SCENE 2

Search for Mr. Hyde

UTTERSON: *(to audience)* Very strange... you see, Dr. Jekyll's a client of mine. And his will says that all of his belongings go to Edward Hyde. Yes! The same Hyde. But, that's not the strange part; no... it's how it's worded, "Dr. Jekyll's disappearance or unexplained absence."

NARRATOR: *(to audience)* With this thought, Utterson decided he would stalk the mysterious man!

UTTERSON: If he be Mr. Hyde... I shall be Mr. Seek.

(enter LANYON)

NARRATOR: Dr. Lanyon. An old college friend of Utterson and Jekyll.

UTTERSON: Hello, Lanyon.

LANYON: Hello, Utterson! *(they shake hands)* What brings you around here?

UTTERSON: You and I must be the two oldest friends that Jekyll has?

LANYON: I suppose we are. And what of that? I see little of him now.

UTTERSON: Did you ever come across a protégé of his, one Hyde?

LANYON: Hyde? No. Never heard of him. As for Jekyll, he began to go wrong, wrong in the mind. He kept talking nonsense, unscientific balderdash!

UTTERSON: Well, that is very interesting. Thank you, Lanyon.

LANYON: Hmmm... Perhaps I should stop by and say hi to our old friend. Goodbye, Utterson.

(LANYON exits)

UTTERSON: Goodbye. *(looks around)* Now, where is Hyde hiding?

NARRATOR: And they meet...

(enter HYDE)

UTTERSON: Mr. Hyde, I think?

HYDE: *(taken aback, and hisses)* That is my name. What's your issue?

UTTERSON: I am looking for Dr. Jekyll.

HYDE: He's not here.

UTTERSON: Let me see your face, sir.

HYDE: Why? Tell me how you know of me?

UTTERSON: We have common friends.

HYDE: *(snarls)* LIAR!!! *(suddenly exits)*

UTTERSON: Rude! *(to audience)* Did you see that murderous mixture of timidity and boldness? He seemed hardly human. I need to see Dr. Jekyll! *(walks across stage; knocks on door; POOLE enters)* Hello Poole, is Dr. Jekyll in?

POOLE: I'm sorry sir, but Dr. Jekyll is out.

UTTERSON: What can you tell me about Edward Hyde? I see he has a key to the back room.

POOLE: Ah, yes. Mr. Hyde has a key. We have orders to obey him.

UTTERSON: Thank you.

POOLE: Good day, sir. *(POOLE exits)*

UTTERSON: *(to audience)* That evil Hyde definitely has secrets of his own, black secrets. What has Jekyll gotten himself into?

(UTTERSON exits)

ACT 1 SCENE 3
Dr. Jekyll Was Quite at Ease

(enter DR. JEKYLL and UTTERSON)

NARRATOR: Soon, Dr. Jekyll hosted a party, and Utterson was determined to question his dear old friend...

JEKYLL: Thank you for coming to my pleasant dinner party. I always enjoy your company, Mr. Utterson.

UTTERSON: I've been wanting to speak to you, Jekyll. You know that will of yours?

JEKYLL: You are unfortunate in such a client. I never saw a man so distressed as you were by my will.

UTTERSON: You know I never approved of it.

JEKYLL: Yes, you have told me so.

UTTERSON: Well, I tell you again. Because I have learned more of young Hyde. What I heard was abominable.

JEKYLL: *(surprised)* Listen to me. DROP THIS. You do not understand my position.

UTTERSON: Jekyll, I am a man to be trusted. I am a lawyer. *(NARRATOR starts laughing; to NARRATOR)* Don't laugh.

NARRATOR: Sorry, you said "trust" and "lawyer" in the same sentence. And...yeah... My bad. Go on.

UTTERSON: *(to JEKYLL)* Tell me in confidence and I can get you out of it.

JEKYLL: I can be rid of Mr. Hyde when I choose. This is a private matter, and I beg of you to let it sleep.

UTTERSON: Fine, I will let it go... for now.

JEKYLL: Good.

(JEKYLL and UTTERSON exit)

ACT 2 SCENE 1
The Carew Murder Case

NARRATOR: One year later, on a quiet and beautiful London night.

(enter HYDE, with cane, who spooks NARRATOR and addresses audience; NARRATOR frantically runs off stage

HYDE: That guy's rather boring, don't you agree? Let's light my great flame of anger a bit. Meet Carew... an old, OLD guy who is sooooo slow!

(NARRATOR enters dressed as old, old slow guy)

NARRATOR: *(slowly)* Excuse me, can you tell me how to get to the station?

HYDE: Ahhh... no.

NARRATOR: You see I'm a bit lost and can't quite read this map. Here, let me show you. *(pulls out map but can't seem to do it fast enough for HYDE)*

HYDE: *(impatient, rolls eyes, checks watch, finally opens map)* I must go! What part of 'no' don't you understand?

NARRATOR: Here... the station here... *(talking to self)* or is it here? Maybe here?

HYDE: *(getting very angry and agitated)* Old man, you are bothering me! Now move out of my way or die!

NARRATOR: Here it is! *(shoves map towards HYDE)*

HYDE: No... HERE it is! *(hits NARRATOR with cane)*

NARRATOR: *(in his own voice)* Ouch! *(changes to old voice)* I mean, 'ouch'!

HYDE: You're annoying and need to die! *(hits NARRATOR again and drops cane)*

NARRATOR: What?! Noooooo.....

(NARRATOR dies; HYDE runs off very crazy and agitated; NARRATOR looks around then takes off old man costume and leaves it on the ground; UTTERSON enters and examines CAREW'S body – the costume)

NARRATOR: Mr. Utterson, do you know who this is?

UTTERSON: Unfortunately, I do. It's the politician, Sir Danvers Carew.

NARRATOR: Oh, that's bad. Look, here is the murder weapon. *(shows cane)*

UTTERSON: How do you know?

NARRATOR: Cause it really hurt... uhhh, I mean because it has blood on it? Have you seen it before?

UTTERSON: Oh my, yes I have. I gave this to Dr. Jekyll many years ago. I know EXACTLY who the murderer is. Mr. Hyde is the murderer.

NARRATOR: The creepy guy that trampled the girl and has a haunting sense of unexpressed deformity?

UTTERSON: Yes, that's him. Time to talk with Jekyll.

NARRATOR: Yes, let's!

UTTERSON: Ummm... not "let's". You. Over there. *(points to corner)*

NARRATOR: Right. Sorry. It's just getting so exciting, being an investigator, catching a murderer. So much suspense!

UTTERSON: OVER. THERE.

NARRATOR: Got it! *(slowly moves over to corner while mocking UTTERSON to audience)*

ACT 2 SCENE 2
Incident of the Letter

(HYDE enters and sits with an audience member)

HYDE: This will be good, I've got them all fooled!

NARRATOR: Hey!

HYDE: Ah, ahh... Shhh... they can't see me. And, if you say anything, I'll ahh... add you to the body count. Got me?

NARRATOR: See who? I don't see ANYONE except Utterson joining the sick looking Dr. Jekyll.

(enter UTTERSON; DR. JEKYLL is sitting on the opposite side of stage)

UTTERSON: Jekyll, you look awful, deathly sick.

JEKYLL: Yes.

HYDE: *(to audience member)* He does, doesn't he? Ha, hah!

UTTERSON: You have heard the news?

JEKYLL: Yes, I have.

HYDE: *(getting excited)* Here it comes!

UTTERSON: I need to know. You have not been mad enough to hide Hyde, have you? ...You?

JEKYLL: Me? Me?! No. No! Listen carefully. HE. IS. GONE. Mark my words, he will never more be heard of. You see... he left this letter. *(hands letter to UTTERSON)*

UTTERSON: It says...

(UTTERSON reading as HYDE jumps up center stage and faces audience)

HYDE: It says, "I'm escaping, bye, bye. Oh, and the doctor is safe. Signed, Edward Hyde." And BOOM! Those fools think I'm gone! Ta-ta! *(HYDE runs offstage laughing evilly)*

NARRATOR: *(to audience)* Strange dude.

HYDE: *(pops up behind NARRATOR, scaring him)* I am, aren't I! *(exits laughing evilly again)*

UTTERSON: Hmmm...

JEKYLL: I have lost confidence in myself. I am the most miserable human.

UTTERSON: Easy there. Get some rest. I'll see myself to the door. Goodnight.

JEKYLL: Goodnight.

(JEKYLL exits; UTTERSON walks to POOLE as he enters)

UTTERSON: Question, who delivered the letter today?

POOLE: There was no delivery today, sir.

UTTERSON: None?

POOLE: Nothing, sir.

UTTERSON: Thank you. *(POOLE exits)* Well, that's strange. How did the letter get here? Did Henry Jekyll forge for a murderer?! *(to audience)* Oooh, this is getting interesting!

NARRATOR: He has no idea!

(UTTERSON exits)

ACT 2 SCENE 3
Incident of Doctor Lanyon

NARRATOR: Good news! It's been four months and we haven't seen hide nor hair of Hyde! Thankfully! Because rumors had it that he was up to all sorts of debauchery! You might say the death of Sir Danvers was more than paid for by the disappearance of Mr. Hyde.

(UTTERSON enters)

UTTERSON: Since then, Dr. Jekyll has regained his health and is entertaining again!

(JEKYLL and LANYON enter and join UTTERSON; NARRATOR joins them; ALL look at NARRATOR and shoo him away)

LANYON: Jekyll, you throw the best parties!

UTTERSON: You really do!

JEKYLL: Thank you. See you again next week?

LANYON & UTTERSON: Absolutely!

(LANYON, UTTERSON, and JEKYLL cheers and exit)

NARRATOR: *(to audience)* The trio were inseparable, until...

(UTTERSON knocks on the door; POOLE enters)

POOLE: Hello, Mr. Utterson. Dr. Jekyll is confined to the house and is seeing no one. Good day.

(POOLE exits)

UTTERSON: Ok, that's weird. I'll try again tomorrow.

(POOLE enters)

POOLE: Nope. He still does not want to see you. And, please do not come back tomorrow or the next. Good day.

UTTERSON: What about...

POOLE: No. Good. Day.

(POOLE exits)

UTTERSON: *(mocks him)* Good day! Hmph! I know! Lanyon.

(LANYON enters looking deathly ill)

LANYON: Hello, Utterson. I don't feel well.

UTTERSON: Or look well. It's almost as if you have a death-warrant written upon your face.

LANYON: I am a doomed man. I have had a shock, and I shall never recover.

UTTERSON: Jekyll is ill, too. Have you seen him?

LANYON: Stop. I am quite done with that person.

UTTERSON: That's rather harsh, don't you think? We are very old friends, we shall not live to make others.

LANYON: I'm good with that. My days are numbered anyway.

(LANYON exits)

UTTERSON: That makes me mad. I need to write Jekyll. *(pulls out paper, writes, hands to NARRATOR to deliver)*

NARRATOR: *(reading)* Dear Jekyll, you're being a meany. Stop it! *(to audience)* Oh, snap! *(delivers offstage; pause, JEKYLL enters and hands letter to UTTERSON, then addresses the audience; UTTERSON acts as if he is reading the letter)*

JEKYLL: Dear Utterson, I received your angry letter. Boo-hoo. Get over it. The quarrel with Lanyon is incurable.

NARRATOR: Ouch!

JEKYLL: Achem... Going forward, my door will be shut even to you.

UTTERSON: What!?

JEKYLL: I must go my own dark way. But, I do ask one last favor, and that is to respect my silence. *(JEKYLL exits)*

UTTERSON: This guy is a piece of work.

NARRATOR: Right?

UTTERSON: Shut it!

NARRATOR: Right!

(LANYON enters)

LANYON: I'm dead now. *(hands UTTERSON an envelope)* Here, read this. *(LANYON falls over dead; NARRATOR checks body)*

NARRATOR: Yep. Look at his face. Death by shock!

UTTERSON: *(reads envelope)* PRIVATE: for the hands of Utterson ALONE. *(opens envelope to find another envelope)* "not to be opened till the death or disappearance of Dr. Jekyll." Really?! You two are killing me!

(ALL exit except NARRATOR)

ACT 3 SCENE 1
Incident at the Window

(enter UTTERSON)

NARRATOR: Thanks for inviting me to walk!

UTTERSON: Well, my other two best friends are basically dead, so I guess you'll do.

NARRATOR: Thanks?

UTTERSON: Hey look, there's the door we started the play with. I think Mr. Hyde is gone for good.

NARRATOR: Ummm... considering we're still on stage, probably not.

UTTERSON: Good point. Oh look, it's Jekyll!

(JEKYLL appears at the edge of stage)

UTTERSON: Jekyll, I trust you are better!

JEKYLL: Actually, I'm not. I will not last long.

NARRATOR: He's cheery.

UTTERSON: Come on out. Join us.

JEKYLL: I would love to, but I can't. Just seeing you makes me smile.

(JEKYLL smiles; and then suddenly his face and body contort with looks of terror and despair; JEKYLL quickly exits; UTTERSON and NARRATOR are shocked and scared; they slowly walk around stage without talking for a bit)

NARRATOR: *(dazed)* What was...

UTTERSON: I-I... I... don't...

NARRATOR: I'm freaking out, man. *(starts panicking)*

UTTERSON: *(grabs NARRATOR on the shoulders)* HEY! Stop! What are you doing?

NARRATOR: Panicking, isn't it a bit obvious?!

UTTERSON: You don't panic like that. THIS is how you panic!!!

(runs around crazy and screaming, NARRATOR watches UTTERSON and panics the same way as he exits)

ACT 3 SCENE 2
The Last Night

(NARRATOR enters)

NARRATOR: Well, that was quite an experience! About a week later, Utterson decided to confront Jekyll.

(UTTERSON and POOLE enter)

POOLE: Mr. Utterson, I'm so glad you are here. There's the doctor's office. Listen carefully. *(POOLE knocks on door)* Mr. Utterson, sir, asking to see you.

HYDE: *(from backstage)* Tell him I cannot see anyone.

POOLE: *(to UTTERSON)* See! That's not my master's voice! It's NOT him!!! And he has been crying night after night for some sort of medicine.

UTTERSON: Crying?

POOLE: He sends me to see chemists at least twice a day and it's never, "the right stuff"!

HYDE: *(from backstage)* No, it's not!!!

POOLE: See!

UTTERSON: Ok, that is odd. But, supposing Dr. Jekyll to have been, well... murdered, why would the killer stay here for eight days?

NARRATOR: Oohh... facts in your face! What do you say to that?!

POOLE: Well... I've seen HIM!!!

UTTERSON: WHAT?! Why didn't you lead with THAT?!

POOLE: *(motions to audience)* To build the suspense.

UTTERSON: Oh. Ok. Go on.

POOLE: A few days ago, I came into the large room and saw HIM! He whipped upstairs and cried out like a rat! He was UGLY and more of a dwarf.

UTTERSON: Well then, we are going to break in that door!

POOLE: Now that's talking!

UTTERSON: Poole, before we go in, I need to know, did you recognize this creature?

POOLE: If you mean, was it Mr. Hyde? Why, yes, I think it was!

UTTERSON: Well, that monster scares the bejeebers out of me!

POOLE: Yes! Chills went down my spine like ice.

(NARRATOR hides behind UTTERSON who shoos him to the side of stage)

UTTERSON: Ok, Poole, let's do this.

(a door moves to center stage; on one side, UTTERSON and POOLE, on the other, HYDE, pacing nervously)

UTTERSON: *(yelling through the door)* Jekyll, I demand to see you.

NARRATOR: He's not answering.

UTTERSON: Really? I didn't notice! *(to door)* I give you fair warning, our suspicions are aroused, and I must and shall see you.

HYDE: Utterson, please, have mercy!

UTTERSON: Ah, that's not Jekyll's voice, it's Hyde's! Down with the door, Poole!

(POOLE starts to break down door)

HYDE: No! No! No!!! Please, No!!!!

(as POOLE breaks down door, HYDE cries out like an animal, leaves an envelope, drinks vial, and dies; UTTERSON and POOLE enter; they see HYDE'S body, twitching)

UTTERSON: We have come too late. He's dead.

POOLE: I don't see Jekyll anywhere, dead or alive. Sir, this envelope is addressed to you. *(UTTERSON opens it and a letter and an envelope fall out)*

UTTERSON: Here is a signed will. And, in place of the name Hyde, it says... me?

POOLE: What does the envelope say?

UTTERSON: "Utterson, read Lanyon's letter before you read this. Your unworthy and unhappy friend, Henry Jekyll."

NARRATOR: Go and read the letters! I've gotta see how this thing ends!

UTTERSON: Very well.

(All exit except NARRATOR)

ACT 3 SCENE 4
Dr. Lanyon's Narrative

NARRATOR: Are you ready for the big reveal?! I am!!! Exciting!!!

(enter UTTERSON)

UTTERSON: *(opens letter)* Alrighty Lanyon, why did you die? *(UTTERSON starts reading; enter LANYON on other side of stage reading over UTTERSON)* I received a registered...

LANYON: ...a registered letter from Jekyll that said; get a vial from his laboratory, wait for a man to arrive at my door, and give it to him.

UTTERSON: Did you do it?

LANYON: Keep reading...

UTTERSON: If you don't, I will die! Signed your friend, Jekyll.

LANYON: So, yeah. I did it. *(pulls a bag out)* And at midnight, a strange short man, with his face covered, and clothes much too big for him, knocked on my door... *(there's a knock, HYDE enters, excitedly grabs the bag, and pulls a vial from it)*

HYDE: Do you want to see? Has the greed of curiosity come over you? It shall be done as you decide.

LANYON: Yeah, I want to see this!

HYDE: Very well! *(pulls off hood)*

LANYON: Aghhhhh!!!! Oh my, gosh!!! You're hideous!

HYDE: Lanyon, you remember your vows. You can't tell anyone! Behold!

(HYDE drinks vial, screams, contorts, gasps, and convulses for a short while)

LANYON: Are you done yet?

HYDE: Hey! This is my moment, just wait... I've got one left! *(more gurgling and yelling and is finally replaced by JEKYLL)*

LANYON: Oh my, oh my! Oh my! Oh my! Oh my, gosh! You're Henry Jekyll!!!

JEKYLL: Yep.

(EVERYONE backstage says, "DUN DUN DUUUUNNN")

JEKYLL: Thanks! See ya tomorrow for dinner? Bye!

(JEKYLL exits; LANYON stands there in stunned silence, shocked)

LANYON: Ahhhhh....

UTTERSON: Are you ok?

LANYON: NO! My life was shaken to its roots. Sleep left me. The deadliest terror sat by me at all hours; my days were numbered, and I died.

NARRATOR: Wow, a bit melodramatic, aren't we?

LANYON: Yes. And I leave you with this, that creature was Hyde, the very murderer of Carew! I'm outta here!

(LANYON exits; UTTERSON closes envelope)

NARRATOR: Well, that's a twist!

(UTTERSON and NARRATOR stay on stage)

ACT 3 SCENE 5
Henry Jekyll's Full Statement of the Case

NARRATOR: And now, the very man who caused all the chaos!

(JEKYLL enters)

JEKYLL: So, are you interested in how I died?

UTTERSON: Well, I'm certainly curious.

NARRATOR: ABSOLUTELY!!! *(to audience)* Are you?

JEKYLL: Then, read the letter.

UTTERSON: Great! Here we go!

(UTTERSON starts reading; JEKYLL starts reading over UTTERSON)

UTTERSON: Dear Utterson, this is my... *(fades off)*

JEKYLL: ... this is my confession and factual representation of what occurred to Dr. Jekyll and Mr. Hyde.

NARRATOR: *(sitting with the audience)* Oh, goodie!

JEKYLL: I grew up with a lot of money and good schooling. My parents expected a lot from me, so, I had to follow all their rules.

UTTERSON: I know how that feels!

JEKYLL: But, I knew there was something deeper and darker in me, that I had to suppress and not tell anyone.

UTTERSON: Oh, so man's dual nature of good and evil?

JEKYLL: Exactly. With my superb intelligence and science background, I believed that I could separate these two pieces of a person.

NARRATOR: Ohhh... that could be very sinister.

JEKYLL: Yes, so I learned. In time, I created a concoction that allowed these personalities to be split!

UTTERSON: Enter the infamous, Mr. Hyde?

JEKYLL: Yes. Not only did it change my personality, but my physical appearance, too!

(HYDE enters)

HYDE: With looks like these, who needs enemies!

NARRATOR: *(to audience member)* Oh, I do not like him! *(HYDE growls at NARRATOR who hides behind audience member)*

JEKYLL: Suppressed for all these years, with no nurturing, no wonder he was short, ugly, and well... that.

HYDE: Hey! I still have feelings... ha, ha, ha... no I don't! That's why I could go out and just be my evil self.

JEKYLL: I don't have to feel guilty anymore. I slept like a champ! I could now "Hyde" my evil personality.

NARRATOR: Good one!

HYDE: I was evil and wicked with no constraints, and I partied like an animal! *(party howls)*

JEKYLL: *(points at himself)* Good.

HYDE: *(points at himself)* Evil. *(sinister laugh)*

JEKYLL: Till one day I awoke as...

HYDE: Me! That's right, I learned to transform without the solution. Life... uh... finds a way.

JEKYLL: Needless to say, I was suddenly terrified. Well, this occurred again and...

HYDE: again... and again... because, well, Jekyll is boring. Everyone knows it's more fun to play the villain!

JEKYLL: He's not wrong there. That's when I started upping my dosages... but, over time, he kept coming back whenever I slept.

HYDE: Can't keep an evil man down!

JEKYLL: Until I transformed in the middle of the day at Regent's Park. I felt horrid nausea and the most deadly shuddering and BAM...

HYDE: There I was! It had been two months!!! How dare he try to throw me away!!! I am everything he wanted to be but would not talk about.

JEKYLL: That is when I brought Lanyon into the picture, poor chap.

LANYON: *(from offstage)* THANKS A LOT!

JEKYLL: Sorry! Anyway, I tried to end this. But evidently, the original compound had impurities, and those impurities are what made it work. So, I could not replicate it. I was doomed at that point! That was my true hour of death.

HYDE: Apparently, mine too! *(looks at Jekyll)* Wimp. *(dies wildly)*

JEKYLL: I lay down the pen and proceed to seal up my confession, I bring the life of that unhappy Henry Jekyll to an end.

(JEKYLL dies)

UTTERSON: Wow. Duality. Good vs. Evil. Murder. Suspense.

NARRATOR: And the butler didn't even do it! Quite a story, don't you think?!

THE END!

NOTES

The 20-Minute or so Jekyll and Hyde for Kids

by Robert Louis Stevenson
Creatively modified by Brendan P. Kelso
7-10 Actors

CAST OF CHARACTERS:

NARRATOR: our funny, all-over-the-place, yet annoying, storyteller
UTTERSON: a lawyer who seeks out the truth
[2]**ENFIELD:** friend to Utterson
DR. JEKYLL: good scientist with one REALLY bad idea
MR. HYDE: evil – does whatever he wants
[1]**LANYON:** friend of Utterson and Jekyll
[3]**POOLE:** the butler
[1]**SIR CAREW:** a slow and really old soon-to-be-dead guy
[2]**INSPECTOR NEWCOMEN:** an inspector
[3]**TRAMPLED GIRL:** a girl that gets trampled

The same actors can play the following parts:
[1]CAREW and LANYON
[2]ENFIELD and INSPECTOR
[3]POOLE and GIRL

NOTE: Both NARRATOR and HYDE are characters that can be improvised throughout the show. NARRATOR is constantly annoying and trying to weave themselves into the story. HYDE takes many liberties, as he does not follow the rules. Be sure to have creative fun with these two characters.

ACT 1 SCENE 1
Story of the Door

(NARRATOR enters)

NARRATOR: Hello, I'll be your narrator this fine sunny Sunday!

(UTTERSON and ENFIELD enter)

UTTERSON: Ummm... excuse me... Robert Louis Stevenson clearly made me the narrator.

NARRATOR: *(mocking UTTERSON)* Ummm... you're excused and ya boring! And, you're a lawyer, like anyone's going to trust you!

UTTERSON: Rude!

NARRATOR: Anywhoo... Welcome to London in the 1800s. As I was saying, it's a fine, sunny, Sunday...

ENFIELD: Well, hello Mr. Utterson.

UTTERSON: Hello to you, Mr. Enfield.

ENFIELD: Want to hear a fun tale?!

UTTERSON: No.

ENFIELD: Ugh! So boring!

NARRATOR: Like I said...

(UTTERSON glares at Narrator)

ENFIELD: Your face is never lighted by a smile. You see that door right there? It has a very odd story.

UTTERSON: You're going to tell me anyway, aren't you?

ENFIELD: We have an audience, have we not?

UTTERSON: Very well, proceed.

ENFIELD: It was 3 am on a winter's morning, and the streets were deserted.

NARRATOR: Oh! Filled with cakes and scrumptious treats?!

ENFIELD: Noooo. One 's', not two. Nobody's outside. Sheesh.

NARRATOR: Ohhh... would have been better with treats!

ENFIELD: Anyway, I saw this man and a young lady walking towards each other. This man ran into her, trampled calmly over and left her screaming on the ground. And then, he started to hobble away!!! Watch! *(HYDE and GIRL enter and recreate scene)*

(NARRATOR grabs HYDE)

NARRATOR: No you don't, get back here! *(HYDE stands there very calm)*

HYDE: Listen, I'll pay you a LOT of money if we can just make this... go away.

NARRATOR: OK!

HYDE: *(hisses at NARRATOR who hides)* Not you! Her!

NARRATOR: Sooooorry, Mr. Grumpy!

GIRL: Hmmm... ok!

ENFIELD: So, this weird looking guy goes in THAT strange door and comes back with 10 pounds of gold and a check for 90 pounds!

NARRATOR: 90 pounds of scrumptious treats?!

ENFIELD: Pounds is what we call money.

NARRATOR: Ohhh... sorry.

GIRL: Thanks! *(GIRL hobbles offstage)*

UTTERSON: Wow, that IS interesting.

ENFIELD: No... what's REALLY interesting is he came out with another man's check. Signed by the very well-known Dr. Jekyll!!!

UTTERSON: Dr. HENRY Jekyll?!

ENFIELD: The very one! It MUST be blackmail. I've watched the door and the only one who goes in and out is that villainous man!

UTTERSON: Do you know his name?

ENFIELD: Goes by the name of Hyde. And there's something wrong with his appearance, something displeasing, something downright detestable.

UTTERSON: Interesting.

ENFIELD: Very! Oh, it's getting late, must leave! Cheerio!

UTTERSON: Bye.

(ENFIELD exits)

ACT 1 SCENE 2
Search for Mr. Hyde

UTTERSON: *(to audience)* Very strange... you see, Dr. Jekyll's a client of mine. And his will says that all of his belongings go to Edward Hyde. Yes! The same Hyde. But, that's not the strange part; no... it's how it's worded, "Dr. Jekyll's disappearance or unexplained absence."

NARRATOR: *(to audience)* With this thought, Utterson decided he would stalk the mysterious man!

UTTERSON: If he be Mr. Hyde... I shall be Mr. Seek.

(enter LANYON)

NARRATOR: Dr. Lanyon. An old college friend of Utterson and Jekyll.

UTTERSON: Hello, Lanyon.

LANYON: Hello, Utterson! *(they shake hands)* What brings you around here?

UTTERSON: You and I must be the two oldest friends that Jekyll has?

LANYON: I suppose we are. And what of that? I see little of him now.

UTTERSON: Did you ever come across a protégé of his, one Hyde?

LANYON: Hyde? No. Never heard of him. As for Jekyll, he began to go wrong, wrong in the mind. He kept talking nonsense, unscientific balderdash!

UTTERSON: Well, that is very interesting. Thank you, Lanyon.

LANYON: Hmmm... Perhaps I should stop by and say hi to our old friend. Goodbye, Utterson.

(LANYON exits)

UTTERSON: Goodbye. *(looks around)* Now, where is Hyde hiding?

NARRATOR: And they meet...

(enter HYDE)

UTTERSON: Mr. Hyde, I think?

HYDE: *(taken aback, and hisses)* That is my name. What's your issue?

UTTERSON: I am looking for Dr. Jekyll.

HYDE: He's not here.

UTTERSON: Let me see your face, sir.

HYDE: Why? Tell me how you know of me?

UTTERSON: We have common friends.

HYDE: *(snarls)* LIAR!!! *(suddenly exits)*

UTTERSON: Rude! *(to audience)* Did you see that murderous mixture of timidity and boldness? He seemed hardly human. I need to see Dr. Jekyll! *(walks across stage; knocks on door; POOLE enters)* Hello Poole, is Dr. Jekyll in?

POOLE: I'm sorry sir, but Dr. Jekyll is out.

UTTERSON: What can you tell me about Edward Hyde? I see he has a key to the back room.

POOLE: Ah, yes. Mr. Hyde has a key. We have orders to obey him.

UTTERSON: Thank you.

POOLE: Good day, sir. *(POOLE exits)*

UTTERSON: *(to audience)* That evil Hyde definitely has secrets of his own, black secrets. What has Jekyll gotten himself into?

(UTTERSON exits)

ACT 1 SCENE 3
Dr. Jekyll Was Quite at Ease

(enter DR. JEKYLL, UTTERSON)

NARRATOR: Soon, Dr. Jekyll hosted a party, and Utterson was determined to question his dear old friend...

JEKYLL: Thank you for coming to my pleasant dinner party. I always enjoy your company, Mr. Utterson.

UTTERSON: I've been wanting to speak to you, Jekyll. You know that will of yours?

JEKYLL: You are unfortunate in such a client. I never saw a man so distressed as you were by my will.

UTTERSON: You know I never approved of it.

JEKYLL: Yes, you have told me so.

UTTERSON: Well, I tell you again. Because I have learned more of young Hyde. What I heard was abominable.

JEKYLL: *(surprised)* Listen to me. DROP THIS. You do not understand my position.

UTTERSON: Jekyll, I am a man to be trusted. I am a lawyer. *(NARRATOR starts laughing; to NARRATOR)* Don't laugh.

NARRATOR: Sorry, you said "trust" and "lawyer" in the same sentence. And...yeah... My bad. Go on.

UTTERSON: *(to JEKYLL)* Tell me in confidence and I can get you out of it.

JEKYLL: I can be rid of Mr. Hyde when I choose. This is a private matter, and I beg of you to let it sleep.

UTTERSON: Fine, I will let it go... for now.

JEKYLL: Good.

(JEKYLL and UTTERSON exit)

ACT 2 SCENE 1
The Carew Murder Case

NARRATOR: One year later, on a quiet and beautiful London night.

(enter HYDE, with cane, who spooks NARRATOR and addresses audience; NARRATOR frantically runs off stage)

HYDE: That guy's rather boring, don't you agree? Let's light my great flame of anger a bit. Meet Carew... an old, OLD guy who is sooooo slow!

(CAREW enters slowly)

CAREW: *(slowly)* Excuse me, can you tell me how to get to the station?

HYDE: Ahhh... no.

CAREW: You see I'm a bit lost and can't quite read this map. Here, let me show you. *(pulls out map but can't seem to do it fast enough for HYDE)*

HYDE: *(impatient, rolls eyes, checks watch, finally opens map)* I must go! What part of 'no' don't you understand?

CAREW: Here... the station here... *(talking to self)* or is it here? Maybe here?

HYDE: *(getting very angry and agitated)* Old man, you are bothering me! Now move out of my way or die!

CAREW: Here it is! *(shoves map towards HYDE)*

HYDE: No... HERE it is! *(hits CAREW with cane)*

CAREW: Ouch!

HYDE: You're annoying and need to die! *(hits CAREW again and drops cane)*

CAREW: What?! Noooooo....

(CAREW dies; HYDE runs off very crazy and agitated; INSPECTOR enters and examines CAREW'S body; NARRATOR pokes head out and slowly comes back onstage)

NARRATOR: *(to audience)* It's Scotland Yard! I'm safe now!

INSPECTOR: Hmmm... no identification. But, there's this note addressed to Mr. Utterson. Hey you.

NARRATOR: Yes sir.

INSPECTOR: Go get Mr. Utterson, will you?

NARRATOR: Excuse me? I'm not your lackey.

INSPECTOR: *(pulls out notepad)* Ummm... and exactly WHO are you?

NARRATOR: I'm the narrator.

INSPECTOR: Name?

NARRATOR: Narrator.

INSPECTOR: So, you're ILLEGALLY in this story?

NARRATOR: Wait a minute... I don't like where you're going with this. How about I go find Mr. Utterson and we just carry on?

INSPECTOR: Sounds smart.

(NARRATOR exits and returns with UTTERSON; INSPECTOR is taking notes)

INSPECTOR: Mr. Utterson, do you know who this is?

UTTERSON: Unfortunately, I do. It's the politician, Sir Danvers Carew.

INSPECTOR: Oh, that's bad. Here is the murder weapon. *(shows cane)* Have you seen it before?

UTTERSON: Oh my, yes I have. I gave this to Dr. Jekyll many years ago. I know EXACTLY who the murderer is. Mr. Hyde is your murderer.

INSPECTOR: Well then, let's try to find him!

NARRATOR: Ah, sir. Apparently, no one has seen this guy more than twice. But, we know he's ugly and has a haunting sense of unexpressed deformity.

INSPECTOR: Eww. Then I'm just going to leave this to Mr. Utterson to figure out! Good luck! *(INSPECTOR exits)*

UTTERSON: *(to audience)* Hmmm... time to talk with Jekyll.

NARRATOR: Yes, let's!

UTTERSON: Ummm... not "let's". You. Over there. *(points to corner)*

NARRATOR: Right. Sorry. It's just getting so exciting, being an investigator, catching a murderer. So much suspense!

UTTERSON: OVER. THERE.

NARRATOR: Got it! *(slowly moves over to corner while mocking UTTERSON to audience)*

ACT 2 SCENE 2

Incident of the Letter

(HYDE enters and sits with an audience member)

HYDE: This will be good, I've got them all fooled!

NARRATOR: Hey!

HYDE: Ah, ahh... Shhh... they can't see me. And, if you say anything, I'll ahh... add you to the body count. Got me?

NARRATOR: See who? I don't see ANYONE except Utterson joining the sick looking Dr. Jekyll.

(enter UTTERSON; DR. JEKYLL is sitting on the opposite side of stage)

UTTERSON: Jekyll, you look awful, deathly sick.

JEKYLL: Yes.

HYDE: *(to audience member)* He does, doesn't he? Ha, hah!

UTTERSON: You have heard the news?

JEKYLL: Yes, I have.

HYDE: *(getting excited)* Here it comes!

UTTERSON: I need to know. You have not been mad enough to hide Hyde, have you? ...You?

JEKYLL: Me? Me?! No. No! Listen carefully. HE. IS. GONE. Mark my words, he will never more be heard of. You see... he left this letter. *(hands letter to UTTERSON)*

UTTERSON: It says...

(UTTERSON reading as HYDE jumps up center stage and faces audience)

HYDE: It says, "I'm escaping, bye, bye. Oh, and the doctor is safe. Signed, Edward Hyde." And BOOM! Those fools think I'm gone! Ta-ta! *(HYDE runs offstage laughing evilly)*

NARRATOR: *(to audience)* Strange dude.

HYDE: *(pops up behind NARRATOR, scaring him)* I am, aren't I! *(exits laughing evilly again)*

UTTERSON: Hmmm...

JEKYLL: I have lost confidence in myself. I am the most miserable human.

UTTERSON: Easy there. Get some rest. I'll see myself to the door. Goodnight.

JEKYLL: Goodnight.

(JEKYLL exits; UTTERSON walks to POOLE as he enters)

UTTERSON: Question, who delivered the letter today?

POOLE: There was no delivery today, sir.

UTTERSON: None?

POOLE: Nothing, sir.

UTTERSON: Thank you. *(POOLE exits)* Well, that's strange. How did the letter get here? Did Henry Jekyll forge for a murderer?! *(to audience)* Oooh, this is getting interesting!

NARRATOR: He has no idea!

(UTTERSON exits)

ACT 2 SCENE 3
Incident of Doctor Lanyon

NARRATOR: Good news! It's been four months and we haven't seen hide nor hair of Hyde! Thankfully! Because rumors had it that he was up to all sorts of debauchery! You might say the death of Sir Danvers was more than paid for by the disappearance of Mr. Hyde.

(UTTERSON enters)

UTTERSON: Since then, Dr. Jekyll has regained his health and is entertaining again!

(JEKYLL and LANYON enter and join UTTERSON; NARRATOR joins them; ALL look at NARRATOR and shoo him away)

LANYON: Jekyll, you throw the best parties!

UTTERSON: You really do!

JEKYLL: Thank you. See you again next week?

LANYON & UTTERSON: Absolutely!

(LANYON, UTTERSON, and JEKYLL cheers and exit)

NARRATOR: *(to audience)* The trio were inseparable, until...

(UTTERSON knocks on the door; POOLE enters)

POOLE: Hello, Mr. Utterson. Dr. Jekyll is confined to the house and is seeing no one. Good day.

(POOLE exits)

UTTERSON: Ok, that's weird. I'll try again tomorrow.

(POOLE enters)

POOLE: Nope. He still does not want to see you. And, please do not come back tomorrow or the next. Good day.

UTTERSON: What about...

POOLE: No. Good. Day.

(POOLE exits)

UTTERSON: *(mocks him)* Good day! Hmph! I know! Lanyon.

(LANYON enters looking deathly ill)

LANYON: Hello, Utterson. I don't feel well.

UTTERSON: Or look well. It's almost as if you have a death-warrant written upon your face.

LANYON: I am a doomed man. I have had a shock, and I shall never recover.

UTTERSON: Jekyll is ill, too. Have you seen him?

LANYON: Stop. I am quite done with that person.

UTTERSON: That's rather harsh, don't you think? We are very old friends, we shall not live to make others.

LANYON: I'm good with that. My days are numbered anyway.

(LANYON exits)

UTTERSON: That makes me mad. I need to write Jekyll. *(pulls out paper, writes, hands to NARRATOR to deliver)*

NARRATOR: *(reading)* Dear Jekyll, you're being a meany. Stop it! *(to audience)* Oh, snap! *(delivers offstage; pause, JEKYLL enters and hands letter to UTTERSON, then addresses the audience; UTTERSON acts as if he is reading the letter)*

JEKYLL: Dear Utterson, I received your angry letter. Boo-hoo. Get over it. The quarrel with Lanyon is incurable.

NARRATOR: Ouch!

JEKYLL: Achem... Going forward, my door will be shut even to you.

UTTERSON: What!?

JEKYLL: I must go my own dark way. But, I do ask one last favor, and that is to respect my silence. *(JEKYLL exits)*

UTTERSON: This guy is a piece of work.

NARRATOR: Right?

UTTERSON: Shut it!

NARRATOR: Right!

(LANYON enters)

LANYON: I'm dead now. *(hands UTTERSON an envelope)* Here, read this. *(LANYON falls over dead; NARRATOR checks body)*

NARRATOR: Yep. Look at his face. Death by shock!

UTTERSON: *(reads envelope)* PRIVATE: for the hands of Utterson ALONE. *(opens envelope to find another envelope)* "not to be opened till the death or disappearance of Dr. Jekyll." Really?! You two are killing me!

(ALL exit except NARRATOR)

ACT 3 SCENE 1
Incident at the Window

(enter ENFIELD and UTTERSON)

ENFIELD: Thanks for doing these walks with me again, Utterson.

UTTERSON: Well, my other two best friends are basically dead, so I guess you'll do.

ENFIELD: Thanks?

UTTERSON: Hey look, there's the door we started the play with.

ENFIELD: Yeah. I think Mr. Hyde is gone for good.

NARRATOR: Ummm… considering we're still on stage, probably not.

ENFIELD: Good point. Oh look, it's Jekyll!

(JEKYLL appears at the edge of stage)

UTTERSON: Jekyll, I trust you are better!

JEKYLL: Actually, I'm not. I will not last long.

ENFIELD: He's cheery.

UTTERSON: Come on out. Join us.

JEKYLL: I would love to, but I can't. Just seeing you makes me smile.

(JEKYLL smiles; and then suddenly his face and body contort with looks of terror and despair; JEKYLL quickly exits; UTTERSON and ENFIELD are shocked and scared; they slowly walk around stage without talking for a bit)

ENFIELD: *(dazed)* What was...

UTTERSON: I-I... I... don't...

ENFIELD: I'm freaking out, man. *(starts panicking)*

NARRATOR: *(grabs ENFIELD on the shoulders)* HEY! Stop! What are you doing?

ENFIELD: Panicking!

NARRATOR: You don't panic like that. THIS is how you panic!!!

(runs around crazy and screaming, motions for them to panic; ENFIELD and UTTERSON panic the same way as they exit)

ACT 3 SCENE 2
The Last Night

NARRATOR: About a week later, Utterson decided to confront Jekyll.

(UTTERSON and POOLE enter)

POOLE: Mr. Utterson, I'm so glad you are here. There's the doctor's office. Listen carefully. *(POOLE knocks on door)* Mr. Utterson, sir, asking to see you.

HYDE: *(from backstage)* Tell him I cannot see anyone.

POOLE: *(to UTTERSON)* See! That's not my master's voice! It's NOT him!!! And he has been crying night after night for some sort of medicine.

UTTERSON: Crying?

POOLE: He sends me to see chemists at least twice a day and it's never, "the right stuff"!

HYDE: *(from backstage)* No, it's not!!!

POOLE: See!

UTTERSON: Ok, that is odd. But, supposing Dr. Jekyll to have been, well... murdered, why would the killer stay here for eight days?

NARRATOR: Oohh... facts in your face! What do you say to that?!

POOLE: Well... I've seen HIM!!!

UTTERSON: WHAT?! Why didn't you lead with THAT?!

POOLE: *(motions to audience)* To build the suspense.

UTTERSON: Oh. Ok. Go on.

POOLE: A few days ago, I came into the large room and saw HIM! He whipped upstairs and cried out like a rat! He was UGLY and more of a dwarf.

UTTERSON: Well then, we are going to break in that door!

POOLE: Now that's talking!

UTTERSON: Poole, before we go in, I need to know, did you recognize this creature?

POOLE: If you mean, was it Mr. Hyde? Why, yes, I think it was!

UTTERSON: Well, that monster scares the bejeebers out of me!

POOLE: Yes! Chills went down my spine like ice.

(NARRATOR hides behind UTTERSON who shoos him to the side of stage)

UTTERSON: Ok, Poole, let's do this.

(a door moves to center stage; on one side, UTTERSON and POOLE, on the other, HYDE, pacing nervously)

UTTERSON: *(yelling through the door)* Jekyll, I demand to see you.

NARRATOR: He's not answering.

UTTERSON: Really? I didn't notice! *(to door)* I give you fair warning, our suspicions are aroused, and I must and shall see you.

HYDE: Utterson, please, have mercy!

UTTERSON: Ah, that's not Jekyll's voice, it's Hyde's! Down with the door, Poole!

(POOLE starts to break down door)

HYDE: No! No! No!!! Please, No!!!!

(as POOLE breaks down door, HYDE cries out like an animal, leaves an envelope, drinks vial, and dies; UTTERSON and POOLE enter; they see HYDE'S body, twitching)

UTTERSON: We have come too late. He's dead.

POOLE: I don't see Jekyll anywhere, dead or alive. Sir, this envelope is addressed to you. *(UTTERSON opens it and a letter and an envelope fall out)*

UTTERSON: Here is a signed will. And, in place of the name Hyde, it says... me?

POOLE: What does the envelope say?

UTTERSON: "Utterson, read Lanyon's letter before you read this. Your unworthy and unhappy friend, Henry Jekyll."

NARRATOR: Go and read the letters! I've gotta see how this thing ends!

UTTERSON: Very well.

(All exit except NARRATOR)

ACT 3 SCENE 4
Dr. Lanyon's Narrative

NARRATOR: Are you ready for the big reveal?! I am!!! Exciting!!

(enter UTTERSON)

UTTERSON: *(opens letter)* Alrighty Lanyon, why did you die? *(UTTERSON starts reading; enter LANYON on other side of stage reading over UTTERSON)* I received a registered...

LANYON: ...a registered letter from Jekyll that said; get a vial from his laboratory, wait for a man to arrive at my door, and give it to him.

UTTERSON: Did you do it?

LANYON: Keep reading...

UTTERSON: If you don't, I will die! Signed your friend, Jekyll.

LANYON: So, yeah. I did it. *(pulls a bag out)* And at midnight, a strange short man, with his face covered, and clothes much too big for him, knocked on my door... *(there's a knock, HYDE enters, excitedly grabs the bag, and pulls a vial from it)*

HYDE: Do you want to see? Has the greed of curiosity come over you? It shall be done as you decide.

LANYON: Yeah, I want to see this!

HYDE: Very well! *(pulls off hood)*

LANYON: Aghhhhh!!!! Oh my, gosh!!! You're hideous!

HYDE: Lanyon, you remember your vows. You can't tell anyone! Behold!

(HYDE drinks vial, screams, contorts, gasps, and convulses for a short while)

LANYON: Are you done yet?

HYDE: Hey! This is my moment, just wait... I've got one left! *(more gurgling and yelling and is finally replaced by JEKYLL)*

LANYON: Oh my, oh my! Oh my! Oh my! Oh my, gosh! You're Henry Jekyll!!!

JEKYLL: Yep.

(EVERYONE backstage says, "DUN DUN DUUUUNNN")

JEKYLL: Thanks! See ya tomorrow for dinner? Bye!

(JEKYLL exits; LANYON stands there in stunned silence, shocked)

LANYON: Ahhhhh....

UTTERSON: Are you ok?

LANYON: NO! My life was shaken to its roots. Sleep left me. The deadliest terror sat by me at all hours; my days were numbered, and I died.

NARRATOR: Wow, a bit melodramatic, aren't we?

LANYON: Yes. And I leave you with this, that creature was Hyde, the very murderer of Carew! I'm outta here!

(LANYON exits; UTTERSON closes envelope)

NARRATOR: Well, that's a twist!

(UTTERSON and NARRATOR stay on stage)

ACT 3 SCENE 5
Henry Jekyll's Full Statement of the Case

NARRATOR: And now, the very man who caused all the chaos!

(JEKYLL enters)

JEKYLL: So, are you interested in how I died?

UTTERSON: Well, I'm certainly curious.

NARRATOR: ABSOLUTELY!!! *(to audience)* Are you?

JEKYLL: Then, read the letter.

UTTERSON: Great! Here we go!

(UTTERSON starts reading; JEKYLL starts reading over UTTERSON)

UTTERSON: Dear Utterson, this is my... *(fades off)*

JEKYLL: ... this is my confession and factual representation of what occurred to Dr. Jekyll and Mr. Hyde.

NARRATOR: *(sitting with the audience)* Oh, goodie!

JEKYLL: I grew up with a lot of money and good schooling. My parents expected a lot from me, so, I had to follow all their rules.

UTTERSON: I know how that feels!

JEKYLL: But, I knew there was something deeper and darker in me, that I had to suppress and not tell anyone.

UTTERSON: Oh, so man's dual nature of good and evil?

JEKYLL: Exactly. With my superb intelligence and science background, I believed that I could separate these two pieces of a person.

NARRATOR: Ohhh... that could be very sinister.

JEKYLL: Yes, so I learned. In time, I created a concoction that allowed these personalities to be split!

UTTERSON: Enter the infamous, Mr. Hyde?

JEKYLL: Yes. Not only did it change my personality, but my physical appearance, too!

(HYDE enters)

HYDE: With looks like these, who needs enemies!

NARRATOR: *(to audience member)* Oh, I do not like him! *(HYDE growls at NARRATOR who hides behind audience member)*

JEKYLL: Suppressed for all these years, with no nurturing, no wonder he was short, ugly, and well... that.

HYDE: Hey! I still have feelings... ha, ha, ha... no I don't! That's why I could go out and just be my evil self.

JEKYLL: I don't have to feel guilty anymore. I slept like a champ! I could now "Hyde" my evil personality.

NARRATOR: Good one!

HYDE: I was evil and wicked with no constraints, and I partied like an animal! *(party howls)*

JEKYLL: *(points at himself)* Good.

HYDE: *(points at himself)* Evil. *(sinister laugh)*

JEKYLL: Till one day I awoke as...

HYDE: Me! That's right, I learned to transform without the solution. Life... uh... finds a way.

JEKYLL: Needless to say, I was suddenly terrified. Well, this occurred again and...

HYDE: again... and again... because, well, Jekyll is boring. Everyone knows it's more fun to play the villain!

JEKYLL: He's not wrong there. That's when I started upping my dosages... but, over time, he kept coming back whenever I slept.

HYDE: Can't keep an evil man down!

JEKYLL: Until I transformed in the middle of the day at Regent's Park. I felt horrid nausea and the most deadly shuddering and BAM...

HYDE: There I was! It had been two months!!! How dare he try to throw me away!!! I am everything he wanted to be but would not talk about.

JEKYLL: That is when I brought Lanyon into the picture, poor chap.

LANYON: *(from offstage)* THANKS A LOT!

JEKYLL: Sorry! Anyway, I tried to end this. But evidently, the original compound had impurities, and those impurities are what made it work. So, I could not replicate it. I was doomed at that point! That was my true hour of death.

HYDE: Apparently, mine too! *(looks at Jekyll)* Wimp. *(dies wildly)*

JEKYLL: I lay down the pen and proceed to seal up my confession, I bring the life of that unhappy Henry Jekyll to an end.

(JEKYLL dies)

UTTERSON: Wow. Duality. Good vs. Evil. Murder. Suspense.

NARRATOR: And the butler didn't even do it! Quite a story, don't you think?!

THE END!

The 25-Minute or so Jekyll and Hyde for Kids

by Robert Louis Stevenson
Creatively modified by Brendan P. Kelso
9-14+ Actors

CAST OF CHARACTERS:

NARRATOR: our funny, all-over-the-place, yet annoying, storyteller
UTTERSON: a lawyer who seeks out the truth
²**ENFIELD:** friend to Utterson
DR. JEKYLL: good scientist with one REALLY bad idea
MR. HYDE: evil – does whatever he wants
¹**LANYON:** friend of Utterson and Jekyll
²**POOLE:** the butler
¹**SIR CAREW:** a slow and really old soon-to-be-dead guy
²**INSPECTOR NEWCOMEN:** an inspector
³**POLICE:** the police
³**TRAMPLED GIRL:** a girl that gets trampled
³**BRADSHAW:** one of Jekyll's servants
SERVANT 1: another servant
SERVANT 2: and yet... another

The same actors can play the following parts:
¹CAREW and LANYON
²ENFIELD, POOLE, and INSPECTOR
³POLICE, GIRL, and BRADSHAW
SERVANTS can be anyone not on stage *(including you, director!)*

NOTE: Both NARRATOR and HYDE are characters that can be improvised throughout the show. NARRATOR is constantly annoying and trying to weave themselves into the story. HYDE takes many liberties, as he does not follow the rules. Be sure to have creative fun with these two characters.

ACT 1 SCENE 1
Story of the Door

(NARRATOR enters)

NARRATOR: Hello, I'll be your narrator this fine sunny Sunday!

(UTTERSON and ENFIELD enter)

UTTERSON: Ummm... excuse me... Robert Louis Stevenson clearly made me the narrator.

NARRATOR: *(mocking UTTERSON)* Ummm... you're excused and ya boring! And, you're a lawyer, like anyone's going to trust you!

UTTERSON: Rude!

NARRATOR: Anywhoo... Welcome to London in the 1800s. As I was saying, it's a fine, sunny, Sunday...

ENFIELD: Well, hello Mr. Utterson.

UTTERSON: Hello to you, Mr. Enfield.

ENFIELD: Want to hear a fun tale?!

UTTERSON: No.

ENFIELD: Ugh! So boring!

NARRATOR: Like I said...

(UTTERSON glares at Narrator)

ENFIELD: Your face is never lighted by a smile. You see that door right there? It has a very odd story.

UTTERSON: You're going to tell me anyway, aren't you?

ENFIELD: We have an audience, have we not?

UTTERSON: Very well, proceed.

ENFIELD: It was 3 am on a winter's morning, and the streets were deserted.

NARRATOR: Oh! Filled with cakes and scrumptious treats?!

ENFIELD: Noooo. One 's', not two. Nobody's outside. Sheesh.

NARRATOR: Ohhh... would have been better with treats!

ENFIELD: Anyway, I saw this man and a young lady walking towards each other. This man ran into her, trampled calmly over and left her screaming on the ground. And then, he started to hobble away!!! Watch! *(HYDE and GIRL enter and recreate scene)*

(NARRATOR grabs HYDE)

NARRATOR: No you don't, get back here! *(HYDE stands there very calm)*

HYDE: Listen, I'll pay you a LOT of money if we can just make this... go away.

NARRATOR: OK!

HYDE: *(hisses at NARRATOR who hides)* Not you! Her!

GIRL: Hmmm... ok!

ENFIELD: So, this weird looking guy goes in THAT strange door and comes back with 10 pounds of gold and a check for 90 pounds!

NARRATOR: 90 pounds of scrumptious treats?!

ENFIELD: Pounds is what we call money.

NARRATOR: Ohhh... sorry.

GIRL: Thanks! *(GIRL hobbles offstage)*

UTTERSON: Wow, that IS interesting.

ENFIELD: No... what's REALLY interesting is he came out with another man's check. Signed by the very well-known Dr. Jekyll!!!

UTTERSON: Dr. HENRY Jekyll?!

ENFIELD: The very one! It MUST be blackmail. I've watched the door and the only one who goes in and out is that villainous man!

UTTERSON: Do you know his name?

ENFIELD: Goes by the name of Hyde. And there's something wrong with his appearance, something displeasing, something downright detestable.

UTTERSON: Interesting.

ENFIELD: Very! Oh, it's getting late, must leave! Cheerio!

UTTERSON: Bye.

(ENFIELD exits)

ACT 1 SCENE 2
Search for Mr. Hyde

UTTERSON: *(to audience)* Very strange... you see, Dr. Jekyll's a client of mine. And his will says that all of his belongings go to Edward Hyde. Yes! The same Hyde. But, that's not the strange part; no... it's how it's worded, "Dr. Jekyll's disappearance or unexplained absence."

NARRATOR: *(to audience)* With this thought, Utterson decided he would stalk the mysterious man!

UTTERSON: If he be Mr. Hyde... I shall be Mr. Seek.

(enter LANYON)

NARRATOR: Dr. Lanyon. An old college friend of Utterson and Jekyll.

UTTERSON: Hello, Lanyon.

LANYON: Hello, Utterson! *(they shake hands)* What brings you around here?

UTTERSON: You and I must be the two oldest friends that Jekyll has?

LANYON: I suppose we are. And what of that? I see little of him now.

UTTERSON: Did you ever come across a protégé of his, one Hyde?

LANYON: Hyde? No. Never heard of him. As for Jekyll, he began to go wrong, wrong in the mind. He kept talking nonsense, unscientific balderdash!

UTTERSON: Well, that is very interesting. Thank you, Lanyon.

LANYON: Hmmm... Perhaps I should stop by and say hi to our old friend. Goodbye, Utterson.

(LANYON exits)

UTTERSON: Goodbye. *(looks around)* Now, where is Hyde hiding?

NARRATOR: And they meet...

(enter HYDE)

UTTERSON: Mr. Hyde, I think?

HYDE: *(taken aback, and hisses)* That is my name. What's your issue?

UTTERSON: I am looking for Dr. Jekyll.

HYDE: He's not here.

UTTERSON: Let me see your face, sir.

HYDE: Why? Tell me how you know of me?

UTTERSON: We have common friends.

HYDE: *(snarls)* LIAR!!! *(suddenly exits)*

UTTERSON: Rude! *(to audience)* Did you see that murderous mixture of timidity and boldness? He seemed hardly human. I need to see Dr. Jekyll! *(walks across stage; knocks on door; POOLE enters)* Hello Poole, is Dr. Jekyll in?

POOLE: I'm sorry sir, but Dr. Jekyll is out.

UTTERSON: What can you tell me about Edward Hyde? I see he has a key to the back room.

POOLE: Ah, yes. Mr. Hyde has a key. We have orders to obey him.

UTTERSON: Thank you.

POOLE: Good day, sir. *(POOLE exits)*

UTTERSON: *(to audience)* That evil Hyde definitely has secrets of his own, black secrets. What has Jekyll gotten himself into?

(UTTERSON exits)

ACT 1 SCENE 3
Dr. Jekyll Was Quite at Ease

(enter DR. JEKYLL and UTTERSON)

NARRATOR: Soon, Dr. Jekyll hosted a party, and Utterson was determined to question his dear old friend...

JEKYLL: Thank you for coming to my pleasant dinner party. I always enjoy your company, Mr. Utterson.

UTTERSON: I've been wanting to speak to you, Jekyll. You know that will of yours?

JEKYLL: You are unfortunate in such a client. I never saw a man so distressed as you were by my will.

UTTERSON: You know I never approved of it.

JEKYLL: Yes, you have told me so. Again and again.

UTTERSON: Well, I tell you again. Because I have learned more of young Hyde. What I heard was abominable.

JEKYLL: *(surprised)* Listen to me. DROP THIS. You do not understand my position.

UTTERSON: Jekyll, I am a man to be trusted. I am a lawyer. *(NARRATOR starts laughing; to NARRATOR)* Don't laugh.

NARRATOR: Sorry, you said "trust" and "lawyer" in the same sentence. And...yeah... My bad. Go on.

UTTERSON: *(to JEKYLL)* Tell me in confidence and I can get you out of it.

JEKYLL: I can be rid of Mr. Hyde when I choose. This is a private matter, and I beg of you to let it sleep.

UTTERSON: Fine, I will let it go... for now.

JEKYLL: Good.

(JEKYLL and UTTERSON exit)

ACT 2 SCENE 1
The Carew Murder Case

NARRATOR: One year later, on a quiet and beautiful London night.

(enter HYDE, with cane, who spooks NARRATOR and addresses audience; NARRATOR frantically runs off stage)

HYDE: That guy's rather boring, don't you agree? Let's light my great flame of anger a bit. Meet Carew... an old, OLD guy who is sooooo slow!

(CAREW enters slowly)

CAREW: *(slowly)* Excuse me, can you tell me how to get to the station?

HYDE: Ahhh... no.

CAREW: You see I'm a bit lost and can't quite read this map. Here, let me show you. *(pulls out map but can't seem to do it fast enough for HYDE)*

HYDE: *(impatient, rolls eyes, checks watch, finally opens map)* I must go! What part of 'no' don't you understand?

CAREW: Here... the station here... *(talking to self)* or is it here? Maybe here?

HYDE: *(getting very angry and agitated)* Old man, you are bothering me! Now move out of my way or die!

CAREW: Here it is! *(shoves map towards HYDE)*

HYDE: No... HERE it is! *(hits CAREW with cane)*

CAREW: Ouch!

HYDE: You're annoying and need to die! *(hits CAREW again and drops cane)*

CAREW: What?! Noooooo.....

(CAREW dies; HYDE runs off very crazy and agitated; INSPECTOR and POLICE enter and examine CAREW'S body; NARRATOR pokes head out and slowly comes back onstage)

NARRATOR: *(to audience)* It's Scotland Yard! I'm safe now!

INSPECTOR: Any identification?

POLICE: No sir, Inspector Newcomen. But, we did find this note addressed to Mr. Utterson.

INSPECTOR: Great. Go get him.

POLICE: Yes sir!

(POLICE exits; NARRATOR examines body and INSPECTOR shoos him away; POLICE returns with UTTERSON; POLICE talks with NARRATOR aside)

INSPECTOR: Mr. Utterson, do you know who this is?

UTTERSON: Unfortunately, I do. It's the politician, Sir Danvers Carew.

INSPECTOR: Oh, that's bad. Here is the murder weapon. *(shows cane)* Have you seen it before?

UTTERSON: Oh my, yes I have. I gave this to Dr. Jekyll many years ago. I know EXACTLY who the murderer is. Mr. Hyde is your murderer.

INSPECTOR: Well then, let's try to find him!

POLICE: Ah, sir. Apparently, no one has seen this guy more than twice. But that random character over there says he's ugly and has a haunting sense of unexpressed deformity.

INSPECTOR: Eww. Well then, let's just leave this to Mr. Utterson to figure out! Good luck! *(INSPECTOR and POLICE exit)*

UTTERSON: *(to audience)* Hmmm... time to talk with Jekyll.

NARRATOR: Yes, let's!

UTTERSON: Ummm... not "let's". You. Over there. *(points to corner)*

NARRATOR: Right. Sorry. It's just getting so exciting, being an investigator, catching a murderer. So much suspense!

UTTERSON: OVER. THERE.

NARRATOR: Got it! *(slowly moves over to corner while mocking UTTERSON to audience)*

ACT 2 SCENE 2
Incident of the Letter

(HYDE enters and sits with an audience member)

HYDE: This will be good, I've got them all fooled!

NARRATOR: Hey!

HYDE: Ah, ahh... Shhh... they can't see me. And, if you say anything, I'll ahh... add you to the body count. Got me?

NARRATOR: See who? I don't see ANYONE except Utterson joining the sick looking Dr. Jekyll.

(enter UTTERSON; DR. JEKYLL is sitting on the opposite side of stage)

UTTERSON: Jekyll, you look awful, deathly sick.

JEKYLL: Yes.

HYDE: *(to audience member)* He does, doesn't he? Ha, hah!

UTTERSON: You have heard the news?

JEKYLL: Yes, I have.

HYDE: *(getting excited)* Here it comes!

UTTERSON: I need to know. You have not been mad enough to hide Hyde, have you? ...You?

JEKYLL: Me? Me?! No. No! Listen carefully. HE. IS. GONE. Mark my words, he will never more be heard of. You see... he left this letter. *(hands letter to UTTERSON)*

UTTERSON: It says...

(UTTERSON reading as HYDE jumps up center stage and faces audience)

HYDE: It says, "I'm escaping, bye, bye. Oh, and the doctor is safe. Signed, Edward Hyde." And BOOM! Those fools think I'm gone! Ta-ta! *(HYDE runs offstage laughing evilly)*

NARRATOR: *(to audience)* Strange dude.

HYDE: *(pops up behind NARRATOR, scaring him)* I am, aren't I! *(exits laughing evilly again)*

UTTERSON: Hmmm...

JEKYLL: I have lost confidence in myself. I am the most miserable human.

UTTERSON: Easy there. Get some rest. I'll see myself to the door. Goodnight.

JEKYLL: Goodnight.

(JEKYLL exits; UTTERSON walks to POOLE as he enters)

UTTERSON: Question, who delivered the letter today?

POOLE: There was no delivery today, sir.

UTTERSON: None?

POOLE: Nothing, sir.

UTTERSON: Thank you. *(POOLE exits)* Well, that's strange. How did the letter get here? Did Henry Jekyll forge for a murderer?! *(to audience)* Oooh, this is getting interesting!

NARRATOR: He has no idea!

(UTTERSON exits)

ACT 2 SCENE 3
Incident of Doctor Lanyon

NARRATOR: Good news! It's been four months and we haven't seen hide nor hair of Hyde! Thankfully! Because rumors had it that he was up to all sorts of debauchery! You might say the death of Sir Danvers was more than paid for by the disappearance of Mr. Hyde.

(UTTERSON enters)

UTTERSON: Since then, Dr. Jekyll has regained his health and is entertaining again!

(JEKYLL and LANYON enter and join UTTERSON; NARRATOR joins them; ALL look at NARRATOR and shoo him away)

LANYON: Jekyll, you throw the best parties!

UTTERSON: You really do!

JEKYLL: Thank you. See you again next week?

LANYON & UTTERSON: Absolutely!

(LANYON, UTTERSON, and JEKYLL cheers and exit)

NARRATOR: *(to audience)* The trio were inseparable, until...

(UTTERSON knocks on the door; POOLE enters)

POOLE: Hello, Mr. Utterson. Dr. Jekyll is confined to the house and is seeing no one. Good day.

(POOLE exits)

UTTERSON: Ok, that's weird. I'll try again tomorrow.

(POOLE enters)

POOLE: Nope. He still does not want to see you. And, please do not come back tomorrow or the next. Good day.

UTTERSON: What about...

POOLE: No. Good. Day.

(POOLE exits)

UTTERSON: *(mocks him)* Good day! Hmph! I know! Lanyon.

(LANYON enters looking deathly ill)

LANYON: Hello, Utterson. I don't feel well.

UTTERSON: Or look well. It's almost as if you have a death-warrant written upon your face.

LANYON: I am a doomed man. I have had a shock, and I shall never recover.

UTTERSON: Jekyll is ill, too. Have you seen him?

LANYON: Stop. I am quite done with that person.

UTTERSON: That's rather harsh, don't you think? We are very old friends, we shall not live to make others.

LANYON: I'm good with that. My days are numbered anyway.

(LANYON exits)

UTTERSON: That makes me mad. I need to write Jekyll. *(pulls out paper, writes, hands to NARRATOR to deliver)*

NARRATOR: *(reading)* Dear Jekyll, you're being a meany. Stop it! *(to audience)* Oh, snap! *(delivers offstage; pause, JEKYLL enters and hands letter to UTTERSON, then addresses the audience; UTTERSON acts as if he is reading the letter)*

JEKYLL: Dear Utterson, I received your angry letter. Boo-hoo. Get over it. The quarrel with Lanyon is incurable.

NARRATOR: Ouch!

JEKYLL: Achem... Going forward, my door will be shut even to you.

UTTERSON: What!?

JEKYLL: I must go my own dark way. But, I do ask one last favor, and that is to respect my silence. *(JEKYLL exits)*

UTTERSON: This guy is a piece of work.

NARRATOR: Right?

UTTERSON: Shut it!

NARRATOR: Right!

(LANYON enters)

LANYON: I'm dead now. *(hands UTTERSON an envelope)* Here, read this. *(LANYON falls over dead; NARRATOR checks body)*

NARRATOR: Yep. Look at his face. Death by shock!

UTTERSON: *(reads envelope)* PRIVATE: for the hands of Utterson ALONE. *(opens envelope to find another envelope)* "not to be opened till the death or disappearance of Dr. Jekyll." Really?! You two are killing me!

(ALL exit except NARRATOR)

ACT 3 SCENE 1

Incident at the Window

(enter ENFIELD and UTTERSON)

ENFIELD: Thanks for doing these walks with me again, Utterson.

UTTERSON: Well, my other two best friends are basically dead, so I guess you'll do.

ENFIELD: Thanks?

UTTERSON: Hey look, there's the door we started the play with.

ENFIELD: Yeah. I think Mr. Hyde is gone for good.

NARRATOR: Ummm... considering we're still on stage, probably not.

ENFIELD: Good point. Oh look, it's Jekyll!

(JEKYLL appears at the edge of stage)

UTTERSON: Jekyll, I trust you are better!

JEKYLL: Actually, I'm not. I will not last long.

ENFIELD: He's cheery.

UTTERSON: Come on out. Join us.

JEKYLL: I would love to, but I can't. Just seeing you makes me smile.

(JEKYLL smiles; and then suddenly his face and body contort with looks of terror and despair; JEKYLL quickly exits; UTTERSON and ENFIELD are shocked and scared; they slowly walk around stage without talking for a bit)

ENFIELD: *(dazed)* What was...

UTTERSON: I-I... I... don't...

ENFIELD: I'm freaking out, man. *(starts panicking)*

NARRATOR: *(grabs ENFIELD on the shoulders)* HEY! Stop! What are you doing?

ENFIELD: Panicking!

NARRATOR: You don't panic like that. THIS is how you panic!!!

(runs around crazy and screaming, motions for them to panic; ENFIELD and UTTERSON panic the same way as they exit)

ACT 3 SCENE 2
The Last Night

(UTTERSON, POOLE, BRADSHAW, and SERVANTS enter)

NARRATOR: About a week later, Utterson decided to confront Jekyll.

POOLE: Mr. Utterson, we are so glad you are here.

SERVANT 1: Yay! *(one SERVANT hugs UTTERSON)*

UTTERSON: What?! This is very irregular.

POOLE: They're all afraid.

SERVANT 2: WE'RE SCARED!!! *(starts crying loudly; ALL SERVANTS follow; NARRATOR joins)*

POOLE: Hold your tongue! *(SERVANTS hush)* There's the doctor's office. Listen carefully. *(POOLE knocks on door)* Mr. Utterson, sir, asking to see you.

HYDE: *(from backstage)* Tell him I cannot see anyone.

POOLE: *(to UTTERSON)* See! That's not my master's voice! It's NOT him!!!

SERVANTS: Not him!!!

POOLE: And he has been crying night after night for some sort of medicine.

SERVANTS: Crying!!!

POOLE: He sends me to see chemists at least twice a day and it's never, "the right stuff"!

HYDE: *(from backstage)* No, it's not!!!

POOLE: See!

UTTERSON: Ok, that is odd. But, supposing Dr. Jekyll to have been, well... murdered,

SERVANTS: Murder!!!

UTTERSON: ... why would the killer stay here for eight days?

SERVANTS: Eight days!!!

POOLE: *(to SERVANTS)* Shhhh!!!!

SERVANTS: Shhhh!!!!

POOLE: But, I've seen HIM!!!

UTTERSON: WHAT?! Why didn't you lead with THAT?!

POOLE: *(motions to audience)* To build the suspense.

UTTERSON: Oh. Ok. Go on.

POOLE: A few days ago, I came into the large room and saw HIM! He whipped upstairs and cried out like a rat! He was UGLY and more of a dwarf.

UTTERSON: Well then, we are going to break in that door!

POOLE: Now that's talking!

UTTERSON: Poole, before we go in, I need to know, did you recognize this creature?

POOLE: If you mean, was it Mr. Hyde? Why, yes, I think it was!

UTTERSON: Well, that monster scares the bejeebers out of me!

POOLE: Yes! Chills went down my spine like ice. Bradshaw!

(BRADSHAW approaches, scared and nervous)

UTTERSON: Oh, pull yourself together, Bradshaw!

BRADSHAW: Yes, sir. *(still scared)*

UTTERSON: Ok, go stand guard at the backdoor, in case he makes a break for it.

BRADSHAW: Yes, sir.

(BRADSHAW and SERVANTS exit, wailing and moaning; NARRATOR hides behind UTTERSON who shoos him to the side of stage)

UTTERSON: Ok, Poole, let's do this.

(a door moves to center stage; on one side, UTTERSON and POOLE, on the other, HYDE, pacing nervously)

UTTERSON: *(yelling through the door)* Jekyll, I demand to see you.

NARRATOR: He's not answering.

UTTERSON: Really? I didn't notice! *(to door)* I give you fair warning, our suspicions are aroused, and I must and shall see you.

HYDE: Utterson, please, have mercy!

UTTERSON: Ah, that's not Jekyll's voice, it's Hyde's! Down with the door, Poole!

(POOLE starts to break down door)

HYDE: No! No! No!!! Please, No!!!!

(as POOLE breaks down door, HYDE cries out like an animal, leaves an envelope, drinks vial, and dies; UTTERSON and POOLE enter; they see HYDE'S body, twitching)

UTTERSON: We have come too late. He's dead.

POOLE: I don't see Jekyll anywhere, dead or alive. Sir, this envelope is addressed to you. *(UTTERSON opens it and a letter and an envelope fall out)*

UTTERSON: Here is a signed will. And, in place of the name Hyde, it says... me?

POOLE: What does the envelope say?

UTTERSON: "Utterson, read Lanyon's letter before you read this. Your unworthy and unhappy friend, Henry Jekyll."

NARRATOR: Go and read the letters! I've gotta see how this thing ends!

UTTERSON: Very well.

(All exit except NARRATOR)

ACT 3 SCENE 4
Dr. Lanyon's Narrative

NARRATOR: Are you ready for the big reveal?! I am!!! Exciting!!

(enter UTTERSON)

UTTERSON: *(opens letter)* Alrighty Lanyon, why did you die? *(UTTERSON starts reading; enter LANYON on other side of stage reading over UTTERSON)* I received a registered...

LANYON: ...a registered letter from Jekyll that said; get a vial from his laboratory, wait for a man to arrive at my door, and give it to him.

UTTERSON: Did you do it?

LANYON: Keep reading...

UTTERSON: If you don't, I will die! Signed your friend, Jekyll.

LANYON: So, yeah. I did it. *(pulls a bag out)* And at midnight, a strange short man, with his face covered, and clothes much too big for him, knocked on my door... *(there's a knock, HYDE enters, excitedly grabs the bag, and pulls a vial from it)*

HYDE: Do you want to see? Has the greed of curiosity come over you? It shall be done as you decide.

LANYON: Yeah, I want to see this!

HYDE: Very well! *(pulls off hood)*

LANYON: Aghhhhh!!!! Oh my, gosh!!! You're hideous!

HYDE: Lanyon, you remember your vows. You can't tell anyone! Behold!

(HYDE drinks vial, screams, contorts, gasps, and convulses for a short while)

LANYON: Are you done yet?

HYDE: Hey! This is my moment, just wait... I've got one left! *(more gurgling and yelling and is finally replaced by JEKYLL)*

LANYON: Oh my, oh my! Oh my! Oh my! Oh my, gosh! You're Henry Jekyll!!!

JEKYLL: Yep.

(EVERYONE backstage says, "DUN DUN DUUUUNNN")

JEKYLL: Thanks! See ya tomorrow for dinner? Bye!

(JEKYLL exits; LANYON stands there in stunned silence, shocked)

LANYON: Ahhhhh....

UTTERSON: Are you ok?

LANYON: NO! My life was shaken to its roots. Sleep left me. The deadliest terror sat by me at all hours; my days were numbered, and I died.

NARRATOR: Wow, a bit melodramatic, aren't we?

LANYON: Yes. And I leave you with this, that creature was Hyde, the very murderer of Carew! I'm outta here!

(LANYON exits; UTTERSON closes envelope)

NARRATOR: Well, that's a twist!

(UTTERSON and NARRATOR stay on stage)

ACT 3 SCENE 5
Henry Jekyll's Full Statement of the Case

NARRATOR: And now, the very man who caused all the chaos!

(JEKYLL enters)

JEKYLL: So, are you interested in how I died?

UTTERSON: Well, I'm certainly curious.

NARRATOR: ABSOLUTELY!!! *(to audience)* Are you?

JEKYLL: Then, read the letter.

UTTERSON: Great! Here we go!

(UTTERSON starts reading; JEKYLL starts reading over UTTERSON)

UTTERSON: Dear Utterson, this is my... *(fades off)*

JEKYLL: ... this is my confession and factual representation of what occurred to Dr. Jekyll and Mr. Hyde.

NARRATOR: *(sitting with the audience)* Oh, goodie!

JEKYLL: I grew up with a lot of money and good schooling. My parents expected a lot from me, so, I had to follow all their rules.

UTTERSON: I know how that feels!

JEKYLL: But, I knew there was something deeper and darker in me, that I had to suppress and not tell anyone.

UTTERSON: Oh, so man's dual nature of good and evil?

JEKYLL: Exactly. With my superb intelligence and science background, I believed that I could separate these two pieces of a person.

NARRATOR: Ohhh... that could be very sinister.

JEKYLL: Yes, so I learned. In time, I created a concoction that allowed these personalities to be split!

UTTERSON: Enter the infamous, Mr. Hyde?

JEKYLL: Yes. Not only did it change my personality, but my physical appearance, too!

(HYDE enters)

HYDE: With looks like these, who needs enemies!

NARRATOR: *(to audience member)* Oh, I do not like him! *(HYDE growls at NARRATOR who hides behind audience member)*

JEKYLL: Suppressed for all these years, with no nurturing, no wonder he was short, ugly, and well... that.

HYDE: Hey! I still have feelings... ha, ha, ha... no I don't! That's why I could go out and just be my evil self.

JEKYLL: I don't have to feel guilty anymore. I slept like a champ! I could now "Hyde" my evil personality.

NARRATOR: Good one!

HYDE: I was evil and wicked with no constraints, and I partied like an animal! *(party howls)*

JEKYLL: *(points at himself)* Good.

HYDE: *(points at himself)* Evil. *(sinister laugh)*

JEKYLL: Till one day I awoke as...

HYDE: Me! That's right, I learned to transform without the solution. Life... uh... finds a way.

JEKYLL: Needless to say, I was suddenly terrified. Well, this occurred again and...

HYDE: again... and again... because, well, Jekyll is boring. Everyone knows it's more fun to play the villain!

JEKYLL: He's not wrong there. That's when I started upping my dosages... but, over time, he kept coming back whenever I slept.

HYDE: Can't keep an evil man down!

JEKYLL: Until I transformed in the middle of the day at Regent's Park. I felt horrid nausea and the most deadly shuddering and BAM...

HYDE: There I was! It had been two months!!! How dare he try to throw me away!!! I am everything he wanted to be but would not talk about.

JEKYLL: That is when I brought Lanyon into the picture, poor chap.

LANYON: *(from offstage)* THANKS A LOT!

JEKYLL: Sorry! Anyway, I tried to end this. But evidently, the original compound had impurities, and those impurities are what made it work. So, I could not replicate it. I was doomed at that point! That was my true hour of death.

HYDE: Apparently, mine too! *(looks at Jekyll)* Wimp. *(dies wildly)*

JEKYLL: I lay down the pen and proceed to seal up my confession, I bring the life of that unhappy Henry Jekyll to an end.

(JEKYLL dies)

UTTERSON: Wow. Duality. Good vs. Evil. Murder. Suspense.

NARRATOR: And the butler didn't even do it! Quite a story, don't you think?!

THE END!

Special Thanks

To start off with, a big thanks goes to Bradley. He had the original idea of creating the narrator who helped our Mr. Utterson stay more in character. His ideas are always critical and welcome!

Also, a big shout out to Dave Coonan and Malverine Theatre for doing a virtual reading of my beta script and really pointing out some areas of improvement. (which then led to the Narrator)

And as always, a big thank you to all our other beta readers who are ALWAYS improving our scripts! Khara C. Barnhart, Angela Herrick, Jean, Royce, Catherine, Isidro, Rosemary, Jerry, Bridget, Roy, Kayla, Laura, Rebecca, Debbie, Parker, and of course, Kenny! What a great list! Our books are not what their potential is, without our Betas!!!

-Brendan

Sneak Peeks at other Playing With Plays books:

Macbeth for Kids..Pg 96

Frankenstein for Kids.......................................Pg 98

Beowulf for Kids..Pg 100

Dracula for Kids...Pg 102

Sneak peek of
Macbeth for Kids
ACT 2 SCENE 1

(DUNCAN runs on stage and dies with a dagger stuck in him, MACBETH drags his body off and then returns with the bloody dagger. LADY MACBETH enters)

LADY MACBETH: Did you do it?

MACBETH: *(clueless)* Do what?

LADY MACBETH: KILL HIM!

MACBETH: Oh yeah, all done. I have done the deed.

LADY MACBETH: *(pointing at the dagger)* What is that?

MACBETH: What?

LADY MACBETH: Why do you still have the bloody dagger with you?

MACBETH: Ummmmm, I don't know.

LADY MACBETH: Well go put it back!

MACBETH: NO! I'll go no more! I'm scared of the dark, and there is a dead body in there. I am afraid to think what I have done.

LADY MACBETH: Man you are a wimp, give me the dagger. *(LADY MACBETH takes the dagger, exits, and returns)*

LADY MACBETH: All done.

(there is a loud knock at the door)

LADY MACBETH: It's 2am! This really is not a good time for more visitors. *(goes to the door)* Who is it? *(opens door)*

MACDUFF: It is Macduff. I am here to see the king.

MACBETH: He is sleeping in there.

(MACDUFF exits while MACBETH and LADY MACBETH look at each other)

MACDUFF: *(offstage scream)* AGHHHHHHHHHHH – He's dead, he's dead!!! *(MACDUFF enters)*

MACBETH: Who?

MACDUFF: Who do you think? *(they both scream)*

BANQUO: *(BANQUO, MALCOLM, and DONALBAIN enter)* What happened, can't someone get a good night sleep around here?

MACDUFF: The king has been murdered.

MALCOLM & DONALBAIN: Aghhhhhhhh!!!!!!!!

DONALBAIN: We must be next.

MALCOLM: Let's get out of here.

DONALBAIN: I'm heading to Ireland.

MALCOLM: I'm off to England. *(MALCOLM and DONALBAIN exit)*

MACDUFF: Well, since there is no one left to be King, why don't you do it Mac?

LADY MACBETH & MACBETH: Okay. *(LADY MACBETH, MACBETH and MACDUFF exit)*

BANQUO: *(to audience)* I fear, thou play'dst most foully for't. *(MACBETH returns)*

MACBETH: Bank, what are you thinking over there?

BANQUO: Oh, nothing. *(said with a big fake smile)* Gotta go! See ya! *(BANQUO exits)*

Sneak peek of
Frankenstein for Kids

ACT 1 SCENE 1

(enter WALDMAN and VICTOR)

WALDMAN: Victor! Come in! You look so tired.

VICTOR: I'm fine, Professor Waldman! I've been working on an experiment. There's so much to be done.

WALDMAN: You remind me of myself as a young student! So few of us are willing to give our right arms for science!

VICTOR: You have no idea! *(to audience)* I will solve the mysteries of creation! *(laughs madly)*

WALDMAN: Pardon me?

VICTOR: I said…ahhh… I need a vacation! Gotta go back to work. Excuse me! *(VICTOR exits)*

WALDMAN: Strange kid.

(WALDMAN exits; VICTOR pops back on stage and addresses audience)

VICTOR: He'd think I'm mad if I told him! I've figured out how to make dead things live again! *(laughs madly, exits and returns with arms and legs)* I've been through dozens of graves and hospitals. Finally, I have everything I need!

(exits, laughing madly)

ACT 1 SCENE 2

(MONSTER is laying under a sheet; VICTOR enters)

VICTOR: *(to audience)* I see by your eagerness that you expect to see how it's done. Ha! If I showed you, you'd be...SHOCKED! Time to become the world's first bodybuilder! *(VICTOR laughs madly as he raises the sheet to hide himself and MONSTER)* To bolt or not to bolt, THAT is the question! *(there's a clap of thunder, then VICTOR yanks away sheet)*

MONSTER: *(sits up in monster voice)* GRR!!! GRR!!!

VICTOR: It's alive! It's alive!! IT'S ALIVE!!!

MONSTER: You never said that in the book!

VICTOR: I know but, it's more fun to say...IT'S ALIVE!

MONSTER: *(MONSTER takes one step towards VICTOR)* GRR!!!

VICTOR: OK!!! AAGH!!! Monster! *(screams and runs to other side of stage)*

MONSTER: Now THAT'S what you said in the book! ARGHHH!!!

(VICTOR runs away screaming, MONSTER takes the sheet and wears it like a cloak, exits)

Sneak peek of
Beowulf for Kids
HROTHGAR and BEOWULF

(enter HROTHGAR and DANES)

HROTHGAR: *(wailing)* What have I done?! I have created a great hall and have put my people in danger! Hopefully, this monster will not come back again!

(exit HROTHGAR; enter GRENDEL)

GRENDEL: *(whistling; addresses audience)* Off to eat some more people! *(knocks at door, someone answers)* Rawwrr!!! I am the monster of evil, greedy and cruel, by the name of Grendel! Prepare to be eaten… again!

(GRENDEL eats some more people, wipes his mouth with a napkin, and runs off stage; enter HROTHGAR)

HROTHGAR: Noooooo! The monster has come back and will probably keep coming back for 12 years before someone comes to help us!

(HROTHGAR and his DANES wail loudly; DANE 2 crosses the stage with a sign that says "12 Years Later"; enter BEOWULF and GEAT SOLDIERS)

BEOWULF: I, the great and mighty Beowulf, warrior and champion of the Geats, servant to King Hygelac, have heard of your sorrows and have come to help!

(ALL stop crying)

HROTHGAR: How did you hear of our sorrows?

BEOWULF: *(leaning close to HROTHGAR, whispers)* Dude, you have been crying super loud for like 12 years, and I'm right offstage over there.

HROTHGAR: *(embarrassed, wipes face)* Oh right. *(cough)* Yes. Thank you for coming to our aid!

BEOWULF: I, the great Beowulf, alone now with Grendel I shall manage the matter, with the monster of evil.

HROTHGAR: Whew, that's a relief! I have been trying to figure out how to defeat Grendel for years and have failed. He's stopped by 4,380 times to feast on us!

BEOWULF: I never fail! I have defeated many a monster in my day! Including a sea monster... which is extra cool.

UNFERTH: Boooooo. That sea monster wasn't even that big!

BEOWULF: Who are you? And YES IT WAS!

UNFERTH: I am Unferth, great warrior for Hrothgar.

BEOWULF: *(to audience)* Obviously not THAT great. *(to UNFERTH)* You are just jealous of my greatness!

UNFERTH: Am not!

BEOWULF: Are too! And I heard you killed your brothers!

UNFERTH: Wow, that's a low blow... but... uhhhhh.... okay fine. I'll hang out right over here...

HROTHGAR: ANYWAY, back to me and MY problems.

BEOWULF: Right. Only with hand-grip the foe I must grapple, fight for my life then. If he win in the struggle, to eat in the war-hall earls of the geat-folk, boldly to swallow them.

GEAT SOLDIER 1: Wait... what was that?

BEOWULF: Sorry, quoting old text there.... I am going to fight Grendel with my bare hands. If I win, he dies. If I lose, he gets to eat all of us, including you!

Sneak peek of
Dracula for Kids
ACT 1 SCENE 3

(JONATHAN enters holding a mirror; "shaves")

JONATHAN: This castle doesn't have any mirrors. Good thing I brought my own.

(DRACULA enters behind JONATHAN)

DRACULA: Good evening.

JONATHAN: *(cuts himself)* Ow!

DRACULA: Did I scare you?

JONATHAN: No. You surprised me, I didn't see you in my mirror.

DRACULA: *(sees cut; tries to "bite" JONATHAN; sees cross necklace; stops)* Take care how you cut yourself. It is more dangerous than you think in this country. *(grabs mirror)*

JONATHAN: What are you doing?

DRACULA: This wretched thing has done the mischief. It's a foul bauble of man's vanity. Away with it! *(tosses mirror)*

JONATHAN: Hey!

DRACULA: Your dinner is ready. I must go.

JONATHAN: Aren't you going to eat first?

DRACULA: I'll pick up someone - errr something while I'm out. *(exits laughing evilly)*

JONATHAN: Later! *(to audience)* How strange! *(looks offstage)* What's that? Someone's crawling on the castle. It's Dracula! Whoa! He turned into a bat! I've gotta get out of here!

(exits)

ACT 1 SCENE 4

(JONATHAN enters)

JONATHAN: *(to audience)* Every door is locked. I can't escape! I'm exhausted. *(sleeps)*

(The BRIDES enter)

BRIDE 1: I'm hungry. Where's Dracula?

BRIDE 2: Yeah! I need a BITE.

BRIDE 3: Someone's sleeping on my couch! *(points at JONATHAN)*

BRIDE 1: He's cute!

BRIDE 2: Let's kiss him!

BRIDES 1 and 3: Ew!!!

BRIDE 2: Not a real kiss. We'll suck his blood.

BRIDE 3: Me first!

BRIDE 1: No, me!

(BRIDES 1 and 3 fight)

BRIDE 2: Stop! *(to BRIDE 3)* He's on your couch. Go on! You're first and we shall follow.

(BRIDE 3 wakes JONATHAN)

JONATHAN: You're pretty!

BRIDE 3: Kiss me.

JONATHAN: Really? Um, I can't, I'm engaged. *(Bride 3 opens her mouth; comes toward him)* Whoa! What pointy teeth you have!

BRIDE 3: The better to...

ABOUT THE AUTHOR

BRENDAN P. KELSO came to writing modified Shakespeare scripts when he was taking time off from work to be at home with his newly born son. "It just grew from there". Within months, he was being asked to offer classes in various locations and acting organizations along the Central Coast of California. Originally employed as an engineer, Brendan never thought about writing. However, his unique personality, humor, and love for engaging the kids with The Bard has led him to leave the engineering world and pursue writing as a new adventure in life! He has always believed, "the best way to learn is to have fun!" Brendan makes his home on the Central Coast of California and loves to spend time with his wife and kids.

CAST AUTOGRAPHS

Printed in Great Britain
by Amazon